Matthew's Dream

For Madeline and Luca

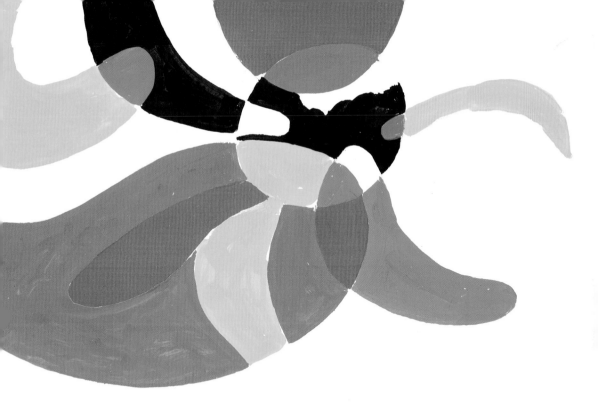

Matthew's Dream

Leo Lionni

Dragonfly Books —➤ New York

A couple of mice lived in a dusty attic with their only child.
His name was Matthew. In one corner of the attic, draped with
cobwebs, were piles of newspapers, books, and
magazines, an old broken lamp, and the sad remains of a doll.
That was Matthew's corner.

The mice were very poor, but they had
high hopes for Matthew.
He would grow up to be a doctor, perhaps.
Then they would have Parmesan cheese
for breakfast, lunch, and dinner.
But when they asked Matthew what he
wanted to be, he said,
"I don't know. . . .
I want to see the world."

One day Matthew and his classmates
were taken to the museum.
It was the first time.

They were amazed at what they saw.
    There was a huge portrait
of King Mouse the Fourth, dressed like a general.
And next to it was a picture of cheese that made Matthew drool.
    There were winged mice that floated through the air
        and mice with horns and bushy tails.
    And mountains and rushing streams, and branches
bowing in the wind. The world is all here, thought Matthew.

Entranced, Matthew wandered from room to room
    gazing at the paintings. There were some
that he didn't understand at first.
    One looked like crusts of pastry, but when he
    looked more carefully, a mouse emerged.

Then, turning a corner, Matthew found himself
   face to face with another little mouse.
She smiled at him. "I am Nicoletta," she said.
   "Aren't these paintings wonderful?"

That night Matthew had a strange dream.
He dreamed that he and Nicoletta
were walking, hand in hand, in an immense,
fantastic painting.

As they walked, playful patches of color shifted under their
feet, and all around them suns and moons moved gently
    to the sound of distant music.
Matthew had never been so happy. He embraced Nicoletta.
    "Let's stay here forever," he whispered.

Matthew woke with a start. He was alone.
Nicoletta had faded with his dream.
The gray dreariness of his attic corner appeared
to him in all its bleak misery.
Tears came to his eyes.

But then, as if by magic, what Matthew saw began to change.
The shapes hugged each other and the pale colors
of the messy junk heap brightened.
Even the crumpled newspapers now looked soft and smooth.
And from afar Matthew thought he heard the notes
of a familiar music.

He ran to his parents' corner.
"I know!" he said. "Now I know!
I want to be a painter!"

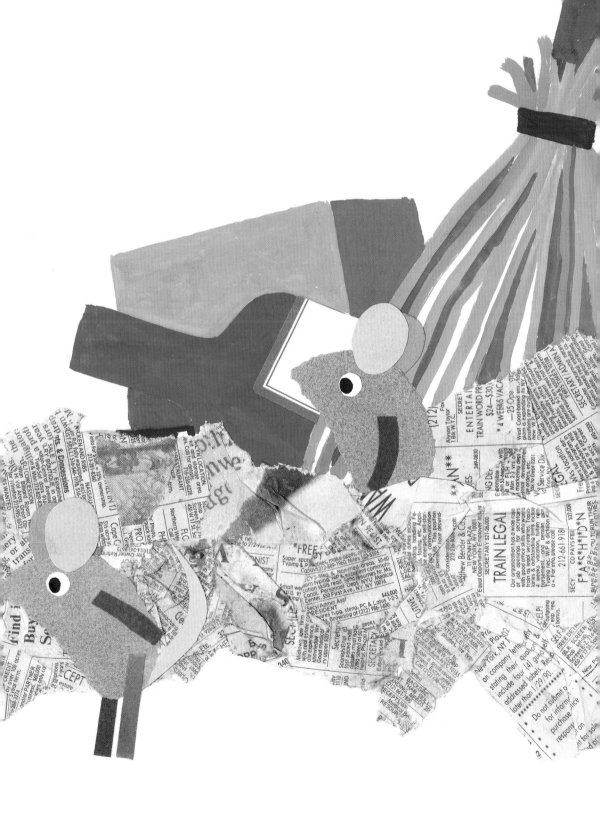

Matthew became a painter.
He worked hard and painted large canvases
filled with the shapes and colors of joy.

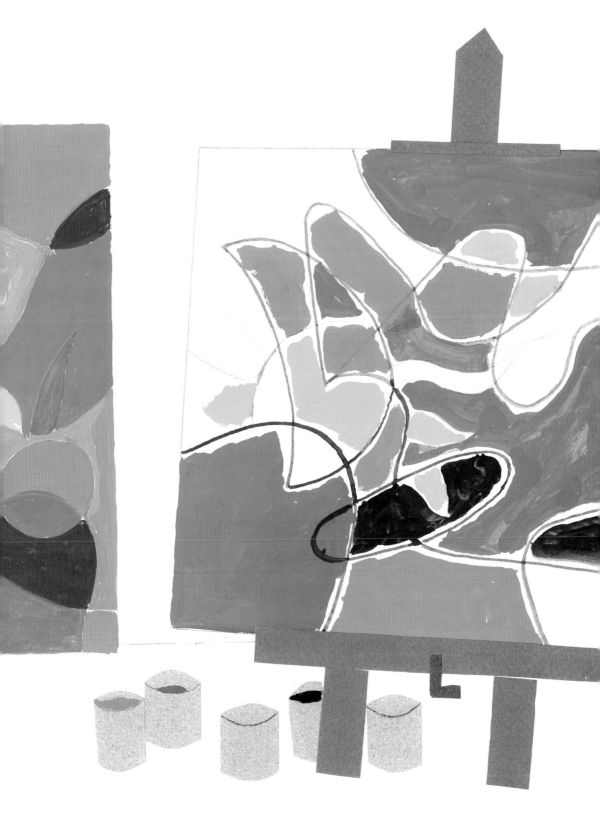

Then he married Nicoletta.
In time he became famous,
and mice from all over the world
came to see and buy his paintings.

His largest painting
now hangs in the museum.
When asked about the title,
Matthew smiles.
"The title?" he says
as if he had never thought
about it before.
"My dream."

About the Author

Leo Lionni, an internationally known designer, illustrator, and graphic artist, was born in Holland and studied in Italy until he came to the United States in 1939. He was the recipient of the 1984 American Institute of Graphic Arts Gold Medal and was honored posthumously in 2007 with the Society of Illustrators Lifetime Achievement Award. His picture books are distinguished by their enduring moral themes, graphic simplicity, and brilliant use of collage, and include four Caldecott Honor Books: *Inch by Inch, Frederick, Swimmy,* and *Alexander and the Wind-Up Mouse.* Hailed as "a master of the simple fable" by the *Chicago Tribune,* he died in 1999 at the age of 89.

Copyright © 1991 by Leo Lionni

All rights reserved. Published in the United States by Dragonfly Books, an imprint of Random House Children's Books, a division of Random House, Inc., New York. Originally published in hardcover in the United States by Alfred A. Knopf, an imprint of Random House Children's Books, a division of Random House, Inc., New York, in 1991.

Dragonfly Books with the colophon is a registered trademark of Random House, Inc.

Visit us on the Web! www.randomhouse.com/kids

Educators and librarians, for a variety of teaching tools, visit us at www.randomhouse.com/teachers

The Library of Congress has cataloged the hardcover edition of this work as follows:

Lionni, Leo.
Matthew's dream / by Leo Lionni.
p. cm.
Summary: A visit to an art museum inspires a young mouse to become a painter.
ISBN 978-0-679-81075-9 (trade) — ISBN 978-0-679-91075-6 (lib. bdg.)
[1. Mice—Fiction. 2. Artist—Fiction. 3. Museums—Fiction.]
I. Title   PZ7.L6634Mat 1991   [E]—dc20   90034242   CIP   AC

ISBN 978-0-679-87318-1 (pbk.)

25 24 23 22 21 20
MANUFACTURED IN CHINA